D0340162

New Pig In Town

Book #1

Story by Lisa Wheeler
Pictures by Frank Ansley

At... eaders
New York ... ey Singapore

Atheneum Books for Young Readers
An imprint of Simon & Schuster Children's Publishing Division
1230 Avenue of the Americas
New York, New York 10020

Book design by Abelardo Martínez
The text of this book is set in Palatino.
The illustrations are rendered in ink and watercolor.
Printed in the United States of America
First Edition
2 4 6 8 10 9 7 5 3 1
Library of Congress Cataloging-in-Publication Data
Wheeler, Lisa, 1963-
Fitch & Chip. New pig in town / Lisa Wheeler ;
illustrated by Frank Ansley. — 1st ed.
p. cm.
"A Richard Jackson book."
Summary: Fitch the wolf and Chip the pig strike up an unlikely
friendship because they discover they have something in common.
ISBN 0-689-84950-8
[1. Wolves—Fiction. 2. Pigs—Fiction. 3. Schools—Fiction.
4. Friendship—Fiction.] I. Ansley, Frank, ill. II. Title.
III. Title: Fitch and Chip. New pig in town.
IV. Title: New pig in town.
PZ7.W5657 Fi 2003
[E]—dc21 2002013239

For Edna Yonek Hess, my lifelong friend
Love, L. W.

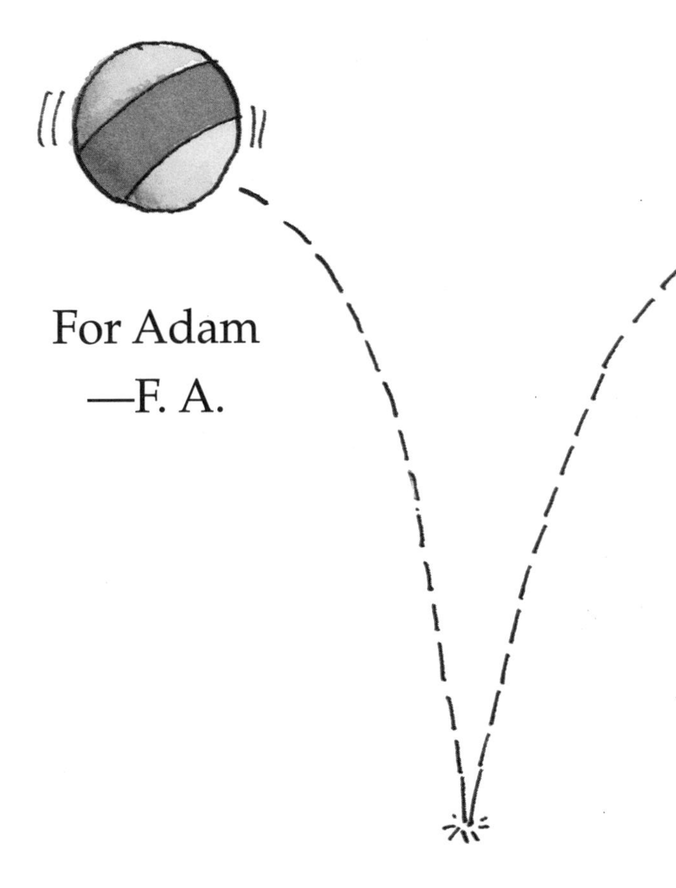

For Adam
—F. A.

Contents

1.

Tap. Tap. Tap.

Chip, the new pig in class,

sat down behind Fitch.

Fitch had long, shaggy fur.

Fitch had tall, pointy ears.

Tap. Tap. Tap.

Fitch felt a tap on his shoulder.

"Are you a wolf?" asked Chip.

"Yes," said Fitch. "I am a wolf."

Chip looked around the room.

Fitch was the *only* wolf in class.

Tap. Tap. Tap.

Chip leaned over Fitch's shoulder.

"What kind of wolf?" asked Chip.

Fitch slumped down in his seat.

He shrugged his shoulders.

Tap. Tap. Tap.

"Are you the big, bad kind?"

Chip asked.

"Are you a big, bad wolf?"

Fitch slumped lower in his seat.

"Shhhh . . . ," Fitch whispered.

"I am not a big, bad wolf.

No talking in class."

Fitch began to chew on his tail.

Tap. Tap. Tap.

"Maybe you are a werewolf,"

Chip said.

"Are you a werewolf?"

Fitch slumped very low in his seat.

Only the tips of his ears showed.

They began to twitch.

"Shhhh . . . ," he whispered.

"I am not a werewolf.

No talking in class."

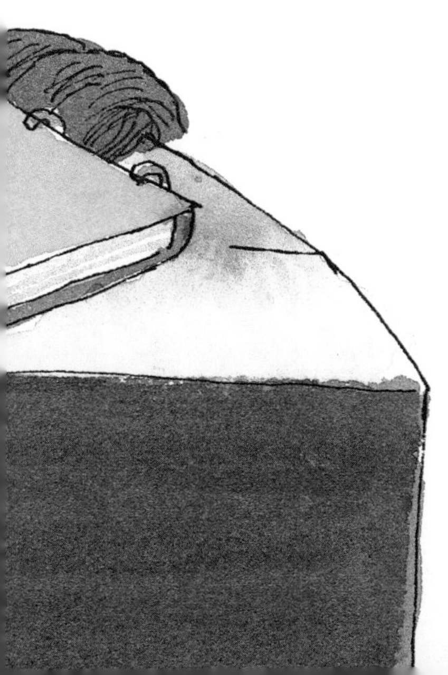

Tap. Tap. Tap.

"If you are not a werewolf," said Chip,

"and you are not a big, bad wolf,

I think I know

what kind of wolf you are."

Fitch's ears twitched faster.

Chip leaned over Fitch's shoulder.

He whispered in Fitch's ear,

"You are a lone wolf."

"Shhhh," said Mr. Hocks the teacher.

"No talking in class!"

Chip stopped talking.

But Fitch's ears did not stop twitching.

Today's Menu
Chicken Soup
P&B Sandwich
Jello with fruit
MILK

2.

Tasty

At lunch Fitch was sitting
all alone.

"Is this your table?" asked Chip.
"It is the school's table," said Fitch.
"I am just sitting here."
"Alone?" asked Chip.
"Alone," Fitch said.

"You *are* a lone wolf," said Chip.

Fitch's ears twitched again.

Chip stood on the tips of his hooves.

He pushed his chest out.

"How do I look?" he asked.

Fitch hugged his long tail.

"You look tall," said Fitch.

"Tall?" asked Chip.

"Tall," said Fitch.

Next Chip lay down on the floor.

"How do I look now?" he asked.

Fitch looked down at Chip.

"You look sleepy."

"Sleepy?" asked Chip.

"Yes," said Fitch. "Sleepy."

Chip took an apple from his lunch bag.

"How do I look now?"

Chip put the apple into his mouth.
He lay down on the floor again.

He closed his eyes.

"You look silly," said Fitch.

Chip took the apple out of his mouth.

"Silly?" he said. "Not tasty?"

"Silly," Fitch repeated.

"You do not look tasty at all."

Fitch's ears twitched.

"But I like the way
that apple looks.
It looks very tasty."
Chip gave Fitch the apple.

"Since I do not look tasty to you,"

said Chip,

"I will sit at your table."

"It is not my table," said Fitch.

"It is the school's table.

I am just sitting here."

"Alone," said Chip.

"With you, " said Fitch.

3.

Thwack! Thump!

Fitch and Chip
were on the playground.
They bounced a ball back and forth.
Thwack!
The ball hit the ground.
Thump!
Chip caught it.

"Do you have any sisters?"

asked Chip.

Thwack!

"No," said Fitch.

"I do not have any sisters."

Thump!

"I have three sisters," said Chip.
"They are all smaller than me.
"Do you have any brothers?"
Chip asked.

Thwack!

“No,” said Fitch.

“I do not have any brothers.”

Thump!

"I have two brothers," said Chip.

"They are both bigger than me."

"Do you have a mother?"

he asked Fitch.

Thwack.

"Or a father?"

Thump.

"I do not have a mother," Fitch said.

"I do not have a father."

Thwack.

"I do not have a sister."

Thwack!

"I do not have a brother!"

THWACK!

"You *are* a lone wolf!" said Chip.

The ball went up, up, up.

The ball came down,

down, down

—*Thump!*—

on Chip's head.

"OW!" Chip cried.

"I am sorry," said Fitch.

"I should not bounce the ball
so high."
"I am sorry too,"
said Chip.
"I should keep my eyes
on the ball."

SCHOOL

Fitch and Chip went back
to their game.
"I have a granny," Fitch said.
His ears began to twitch.
"Do you have a granny?"
Thwack.
"No," said Chip. "I do not have
a granny."

Thump.

"Too bad," said Fitch.

"A granny is good to have."

Thwack.

"For dinner?" asked Chip.

Thump.

Fitch laughed.

"You are a funny pig."

4.

Lone Wolf

After school Chip saw Fitch.

He ran to catch up.

"Are you walking home?" asked Chip.

"Yes," said Fitch.

"Alone?" Chip asked.

"Alone," said Fitch.

Chip sighed.

"I have three sisters

and two brothers.

I never get to be alone."

"Lucky you," said Fitch.

"Lucky *you,*" said Chip.

"I have to do all the chores,"

Fitch said.

He kicked at a pebble.

"I have to share my toys,"

said Chip.

Chip kicked at a pebble too.

"I have no one to play games with,"
said Fitch.
He hopped on one paw.
"My sisters break my games,"
said Chip.
Chip hopped on one hoof.

"Granny knows who to blame when things break," said Fitch. He skipped sideways.

"I get blamed
when I didn't do it," said Chip.
Chip skipped sideways too.
Fitch stopped walking.

"I get lonely by myself," he said.

Chip stopped walking.

"I get lonely too."

Fitch hugged his long tail.

His ears were not twitching.

"You know what I think?"
asked Chip.
"What?" said Fitch.
"I think we're just the same,"
said Chip.
"Two lone wolves?" Fitch asked.
"One lone wolf," said Chip.
"Plus one lone pig."
"Two together," said Fitch.
"Together," Chip agreed.

And that is how they walked home.